The Valley of Little Horses

Fallen Tree

Waterfall

Hawk's Tree

Little Horse on His Own

Little Horse
on His Own

Betsy Byars
Illustrated by David McPhail

An Early Chapter Book
Henry Holt and Company
New York

Henry Holt and Company, LLC
Publishers since 1866
115 West 18th Street, New York, New York 10011
www.henryholt.com

Library of Congress Cataloging-in-Publication Data
Byars, Betsy Cromer.
Little Horse on his own / by Betsy Byars; illustrated by David McPhail.—1st ed.
p.   cm.
Sequel to: Little Horse.
Summary: Little Horse confronts lightning, fire, and dangerous animals
in his effort to return home to his mother and the valley of the little horses.
ISBN 0-8050-7352-3
EAN 978-8050-7352-2
[1. Horses—Fiction. 2. Survival—Fiction.] I. McPhail, David, ill. II. Title.
PZ7.B9836 Lk 2004   [E]—22   2003056630
First Edition—2004 / Designed by Donna Mark
Printed in the United States of America on acid-free paper. ∞
1   3   5   7   9   10   8   6   4   2

Contents

1

Dream

Little Horse slept on a bed of soft straw. He dreamed.

In the dream, he was back in the Valley of Little Horses. He ran in the meadow with the colts.

They frisked. They leaped into the air. Their hind legs kicked out behind them. They neighed with joy.

Suddenly the dream was scary. He heard his mother's long, high whinny. That meant danger. He ran for the cave. In the cave he would be safe.

Little Horse awoke before he got there. He stood up at once. His legs wobbled.

He heard the long, high whinny again. Then he knew the danger was not in his dream. It was real.

He moved shakily to the door of his stable. He looked out. The night was dark. There were no stars, no moon.

The high whinny had come from the stable of the big horses. One of the big horses whinnied, then another.

Little Horse's heart beat faster.

Big horse, little horse, that high whinny meant the same thing.

Danger!

2

Danger

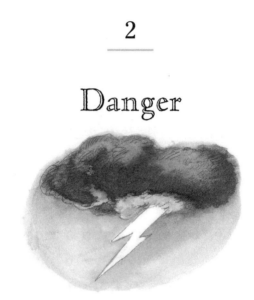

Little Horse had never known the sky to be so black, the air so still.

He heard the big horses whinny again. Little Horse's fear grew.

BOOM!

He knew that sound. It was the clap of thunder. At once the world was white with lightning.

Little Horse began to run around his small

stable. He could not get away from the terrible sounds, the blinding light.

BOOM!

There was only one place he could be safe from a storm. That was in the Valley of Little Horses. That was in the cave, shielded by his mother.

He whinnied with fright. Answering calls came from the big horses.

BOOM!

The thunder was overhead now. The lightning seemed to point to his small stable. To him!

Then came the worst sound Little Horse had ever heard. It was as if the earth was being split in half.

Little Horse reared in fright, his head up, his eyes wild. Then, something huge crashed down upon his stable. Little Horse was thrown to the ground and pinned there. He gave one last whinny, a cry for help, but no one heard him.

3

Green Prison

Little Horse lay where he had fallen. The storm raged around him. There was rain and tiny stones of ice.

The only thing about Little Horse that moved was his heart. It had never beat so fast.

Finally, the sounds of thunder grew more distant. The rain stopped. There was no more lightning. The only sound he heard

now was water dripping from the leaves overhead.

Little Horse found that he could lift his head. He moved his leg. There was room. He began to wriggle through the leaves. Inch by inch he moved forward.

The stable was broken. The fence that had held him was crushed. Little Horse crawled over the pieces of broken wood.

He ducked under a limb of the tree and took a deep breath. The air was cool and fresh. It was like the air in the Valley of Little Horses.

This gave him strength. He fought the rest of the limbs and leaves. With one final burst he was free.

Little Horse stood and looked around him. There was a lot going on. The two-legged animals were running, shouting. To Little Horse's surprise, no one noticed him.

Keeping close to the fallen tree, he made

his way to the stable where the big horses slept.

There, curled up in the straw, with the big horses to watch over him, Little Horse slept.

4

Golden Eyes

When Little Horse awoke, it was morning.

The big horses were being led out of the stable to graze. Little Horse got up. He was hungry, too.

Little Horse did not make it through the door. An animal blocked his way. Little Horse froze.

Little Horse had seen this animal before. He knew those sharp golden eyes.

But the animal's eyes were not on him. They watched the straw on the floor.

The straw twitched. The animal pounced. A smaller animal scurried out of the straw. It darted across the floor and disappeared into a hole.

The big animal reached into the hole with her paw. She felt nothing. She turned and began to lick her paw.

At that moment, she saw Little Horse. Her tail twitched. She took four steps toward Little Horse. She went into a crouch.

Little Horse ran for the door. But, the animal was there before him.

He turned. He darted this way, that way. The big animal was faster.

Then Little Horse saw he was in front of the hole. He remembered the small animal had escaped there.

He fell to his knees and began to wriggle through. He was almost inside when a large paw pinned his tail to the ground.

5

A Rider

Little Horse kicked with his hind legs, hard. His hooves hit the side of the hole, and he fell downward, landing on his side.

He was safe for the moment, but his heart still pounded. As he lay there, he became aware of his surroundings. He was in the nest of the small animal.

But it wasn't straw he was lying on. It was

something soft, something that moved. The animal's young!

Little Horse struggled quickly to his feet. He gave a snort of surprise. One of the young had climbed onto his back.

Little Horse had seen the big horses carry two-legged animals around. Until now he had not known how the big horses must have suffered.

He bucked. The rider stayed on. He came down hard on all hooves. The rider stayed on. He reared. The rider stayed on. Little Horse rolled over. That did it. As quickly as the ride had begun, it was over. The rider lay with the other young. Little Horse was free.

Little Horse poked his head out of the hole. He looked this way, that way. Golden Eyes was gone.

Carefully, Little Horse squeezed himself out of the hole. The way to the big horses was clear.

6

Wild Horses

Little Horse ran out of the stable. The grass was tall. It hid him as he moved to the meadow.

He paused at the fence and watched the big horses graze. Then, slowly, he trotted to the brown horse. He neighed.

The brown horse lifted his head. It was as if he had heard a horse neigh in the distance.

Down here! Down here! Little Horse wanted to cry. He neighed again.

The brown horse took two steps forward. When his hoof touched the ground, it was inches from Little Horse. It left a print in the soft earth.

Little Horse darted away. Now the brown horse saw him. He threw back his head. He snorted.

Little Horse knew that sound. The horses in the valley snorted like that when something spooked them.

The horse reared.

The other horses caught his alarm. They snorted. They began to canter around the meadow.

Little Horse ran for the fence. As he ran, he knew what had startled the horse. He had. *He!*

He had thought of the big horses as his friends. Now he knew he had no friends. Little Horse ran for his life.

7

Fire!

At the end of the day, Little Horse saw a welcome sight. He saw the stream. It ran beside the Valley of Little Horses, his home. But one sad day he had fallen into this stream. It had brought him here.

The setting sun turned the water to gold. It did that in his valley too.

Little Horse found an opening in the roots of one of the trees. He moved inside.

He was careful. There might be a nest with young inside.

It was empty. Little Horse curled up. He slept.

In the morning, Little Horse was eager to be on his way home. He came out of the opening and raised his head. He could not see the sun.

A gray wind blew from the south. It stung his eyes. A strange smell filled his nose. He had smelled this before. Smoke!

An animal darted in front of his tree. Little Horse moved back, but the animal did not notice him. Another animal passed in front of him, and another. Birds flew overhead.

Little Horse realized the animals were running from something. He remembered where he had smelled smoke before. It was the time when the two-legged animals burned a field.

Little Horse caught the fear of the running animals. He ran with them. Fire!

8

The Cliff

Little Horse ran as fast as he could. For a while he found his way by following the other animals.

But, one by one, the animals passed him. Little Horse ran alone.

The smoke was thick. He could no longer see the stream. He could barely see the trees in front of him.

Little Horse struggled on. He was going uphill now, and the way was hard.

A bird hopped ahead of him. It was a young bird. It could fly only a short way at a time.

The way grew steeper. The bird grew stronger. Little Horse had a hard time keeping it in sight.

The bird rested for a moment on a bush. Little Horse wanted to rest too, but he knew he had to keep going.

Then he saw the bird lift its wings, and, gaining his own strength, Little Horse disappeared into the smoke.

Little Horse stopped. He looked down. The next step would have taken him over the edge of a cliff.

The smoke cleared for a moment. There was nothing below but trees and, beyond, the stream. He had to get back to the stream.

Little Horse took one more step and began his long slide to the stream. He turned over and over. He rolled past rocks and bumped into trees.

At last he was at the stream.

There was no smoke here, only cool water, and Little Horse, gratefully, had a drink.

9

Wings in the Night

Following the stream, Little Horse made his way home. He traveled sometimes by day, sometimes by night. He ate grass when he was hungry. He drank from the stream. He slept when he was tired.

There were many noises, and Little Horse kept alert. He held his ears back, turned to catch the slightest sound.

Even so, he missed one.

It was a faint sound, like the wind through soft leaves. Then he smelled feathers.

Before he had a chance to run, wings beat against his body. Talons gripped his sides.

This was Little Horse's greatest fear. The greatest fear of all little horses is a bird of prey.

Little Horse was lifted into the air. Wings beat against him. He was taken higher, higher still.

He looked down. His heart beat as if it would burst from his chest. The earth was far below. The stream, the trees, the hills seemed to be flying past.

The terrifying flight ended high in a tree. For one moment, the grip of the talons lessened. It was his only chance. Little Horse twisted free.

With a cry of fear, Little Horse began his fall to the ground.

10

The Fall

Little Horse dropped to the next branch. The talons were there, reaching for him. He fell to the next branch, then the next.

That was how Little Horse made his way to the ground, dropping from one branch to another. Then, with a thud he landed on the ground.

Little Horse was lucky. The ground was

soft, and his fall was cushioned by pine needles.

He knew the bird was still in the tree. Little Horse buried himself deep in the soft needles and waited. He expected to feel those terrible talons, to feel himself lifted back into the air, but this did not happen.

Little Horse stayed in the pine needles all night. From time to time his body trembled with fear. He did not sleep at all.

In the morning, tired and weak, Little Horse got to his feet. He tried to run. His legs didn't seem to be working well.

He hoped he was going toward the stream, but nothing was clear. He thought he heard the faint sound of water. Was it his stream? Was it only in his mind?

Little Horse began to run. He stumbled now and then on his weak legs. He fell, got up. He fell again.

At last, Little Horse dropped to the

ground. He could go no farther. He had tried his best. The Valley of the Little Horses was too far.

Little Horse lay without moving. The spray from a waterfall covered him with a light mist.

11

Mystery

The mist! The mist came from a waterfall. Could it be THE waterfall? His waterfall?

Little Horse got to his feet. He shook his head, shaking the water from his eyes. He looked up at the waterfall.

He knew that waterfall! He had gone over it the day he had fallen into the stream, drifting far from the Valley of Little Horses until he was lost.

Little Horse wanted to rush up the hill, but he was so close now, he didn't want to take any chances. He stopped to eat some grass. He drank from the stream.

Little Horse felt stronger now. He hoped he was strong enough to climb the steep incline beside the waterfall.

He started up. He climbed rocks. He slipped. He kept going. He fell into a ditch. He climbed out. He kept going.

The thought of the Valley of Little Horses at the top gave him strength. He got to the top, and there it was! Little Horse could see the valley.

His heart raced with joy. Then he stopped. The rushing stream still lay between him and his home.

He knew the dangers. The water could carry him away as it had before. He could be swept over the falls.

He did the only thing he knew how to do. Little Horse kept going.

12

The Valley of Little Horses

Little Horse came to a place where a tree had fallen into the water. He stopped.

Trees had been kind to him. A tree had fallen on his cage and set him free. Trees had given him shelter. The limbs of a tree had saved him from a terrible fall. He would trust this tree.

He climbed onto the trunk. He walked slowly forward.

His steps were small and careful, but his hooves slipped on the wet bark. He went as far as he could, until the trunk of the tree disappeared into the stream.

Little Horse took a deep breath and dropped into the water. He went under. He bobbed up. Little Horse swam for his life. At last his hooves touched ground. It was the low bank where the little horses came to drink.

Little Horse pulled himself up onto the familiar earth. His legs wobbled as if he were a newborn colt. But now he trembled with hope.

He shook himself. Water sprayed in arcs around him.

He neighed. He knew it was too soft for even a mother to hear.

Little Horse threw back his head. He let out another neigh. This time the sound was loud and clear. It echoed throughout the valley. Horses appeared at the top of the hill.

They parted, and there was his mother.

With a heart bursting with joy, Little Horse ran up the hill to join her.

Little Horse's Journey

Farm

Big Horses

Cliff

Little Horse Sleeps

Fire

Stream